Catherine Hyde trained in Fine Art Painting at Central School of Art in London. She is well known for her intellectual and symbolic paintings and manages her own greetings card and fine art print business. She has illustrated three acclaimed picture books – *The Princess's Blankets* (written by Carol Ann Duffy) which won the English Association Award, Best Illustrated Book for KS2 in 2009, *Firebird* (written by Saviour Pirotta) which was awarded an Aesop Accolade by the American Folklore Society in 2010, and *Little Evie in the Wild Wood* (written by Jackie Morris). All three books were nominated for the Kate Greenaway Medal. *The Star Tree* is the first book she has both written and illustrated. Catherine lives with her husband and daughters in Cornwall.
www.catherinehyde.co.uk

For 'Flying Time' with Miles,
Chloe and Poppy – with my love

JANETTA OTTER-BARRY BOOKS

Text and illustrations copyright © Catherine Hyde 2016
The right of Catherine Hyde to be identified as the author and illustrator
of this work has been asserted by her in accordance with the
Copyright, Designs and Patents Act, 1988 (United Kingdom).

First published in Great Britain and in the USA in 2016 by
Frances Lincoln Children's Books, an imprint of The Quarto Group,
The Old Brewery, 6 Blundell Street London N7 9BH QuartoKnows.com
Visit our blogs at QuartoKids.com

Important: there are age restrictions for most blogging and social media sites and in many countries parental consent
is also required. Always ask permission from your parents. Website information is correct at time of going to press.
However, the publishers cannot accept liability for any information or links found on any Internet sites, including
third-party websites.

This paperback edition first published in Great Britain in 2017 by
Frances Lincoln Children's Books, an imprint of The Quarto Group.

A CIP catalogue record for this book is available from the British Library.

ISBN 978-1-84780-673-4

Illustrated with oil pastel and pencil

Printed in China

10 9 8 7 6 5 4 3 2 1

MIX
Paper from
responsible sources
FSC
www.fsc.org   FSC® C008047

The Star Tree

Catherine Hyde

Frances Lincoln
Children's Books

In the still, quiet room in the sleeping house,
the beautiful horse with a golden mane
shines in the moonlight.

Magical.

Waiting.

Ready.

Tick.

The house breathes in.

Tock.

The house breathes out.

It is midnight at Midsummer and Mia is awake.
The night-light has gone out
but the silvery moon shines in.
A soft breeze stirs the curtains.
Mia tiptoes towards the horse.
Outside, in the warm night,
an owl hoots.

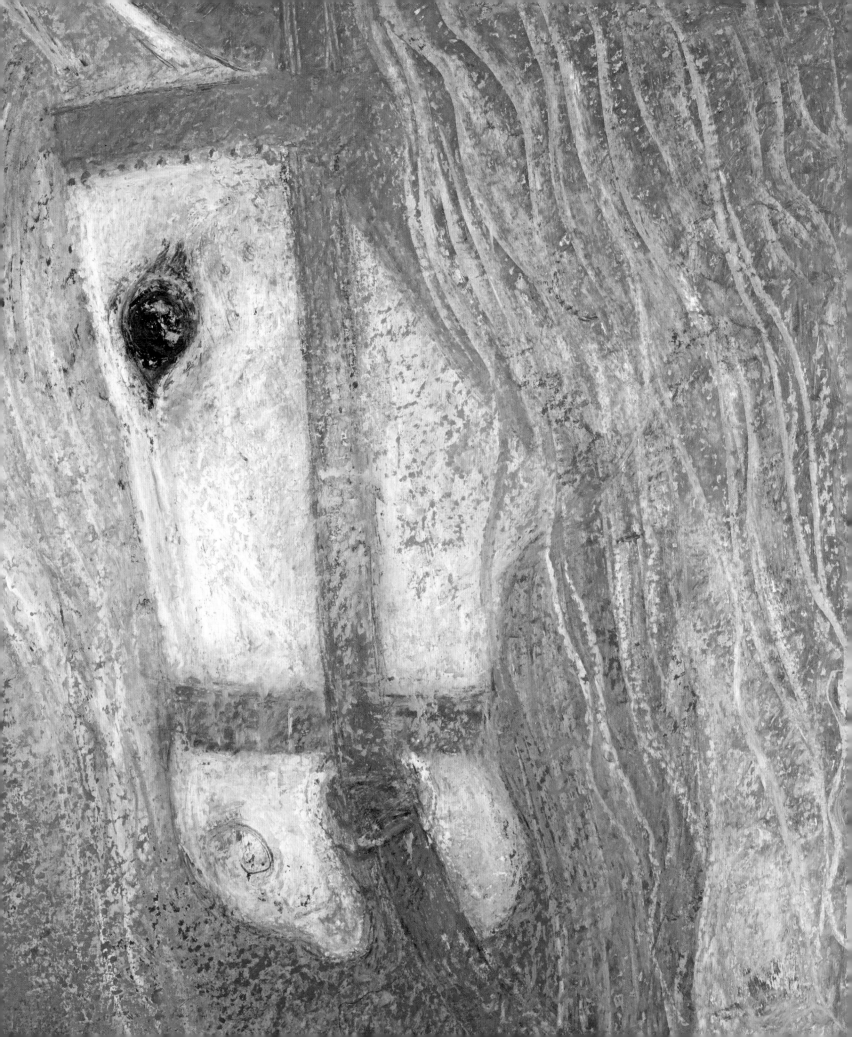

In the dreaming house,
Mia climbs on the wonderful horse
and rocks to and fro, to and fro,
swinging high, swinging low
as she wishes on the
Midsummer Moon.

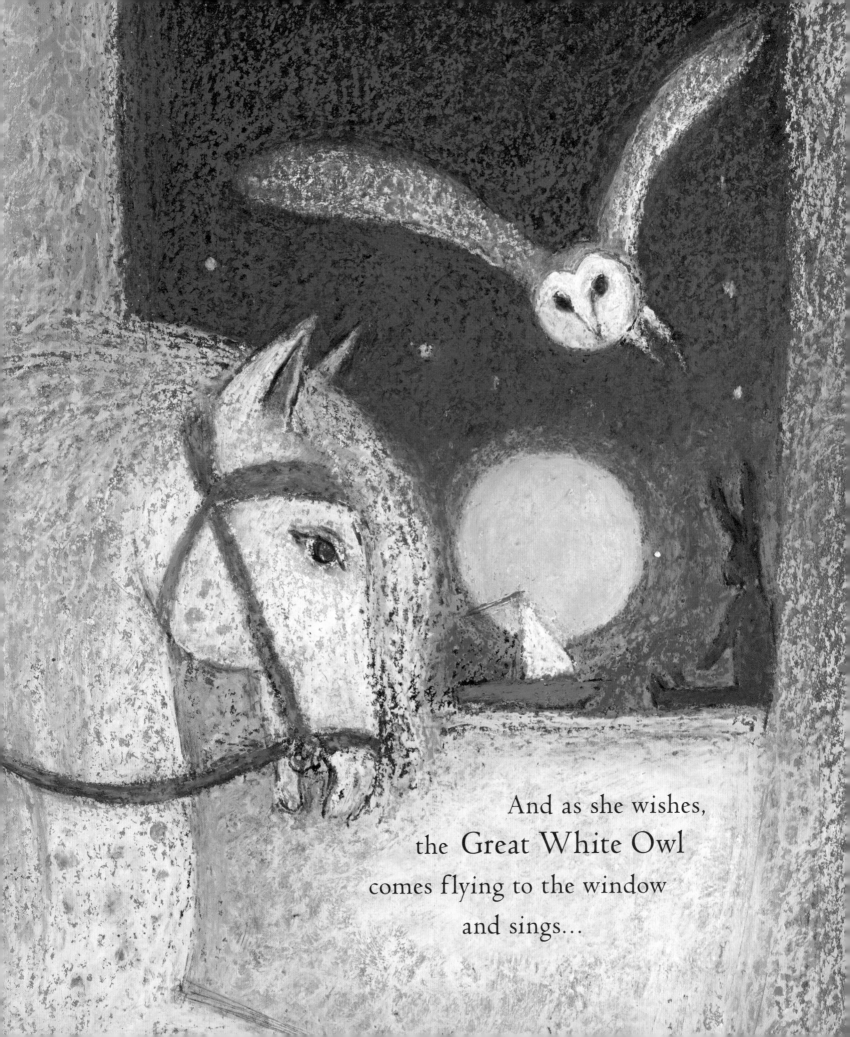

And as she wishes,
the **Great White Owl**
comes flying to the window
and sings...

"Climb onto my back,
Fly away with me,
Over the hills and
Down to the sea.

Sail in the boat with the Little Red Hare,
Over the ocean, over the waves,
Out to the island,
Out to the Bear.

Fly up to the planets,
Up through the stars,
This side is Venus,
That side is Mars.

Away to the north,
Away to the snow
Where the skies sing songs
And the Giant Stag goes.

Climb onto my back,
Ride away with me.
We are looking for the land
With a light in a tree."

Mia and the Owl glide silently
into the velvet night.
Under the big yellow moon
they fly along the tops of the trees,
away from the houses,
away from the shops,
away from the church
where the blunted weather vane
barely stirs.
Over the hills
and down
to the sea.

"Climb on board and sail away with me,
into the night and far out to sea,"
calls the Little Red Hare.

With the wind in her sails
    the little boat goes up and then up,
up and then down,
    over the ocean, over the waves,
out to the island, out to the Bear.

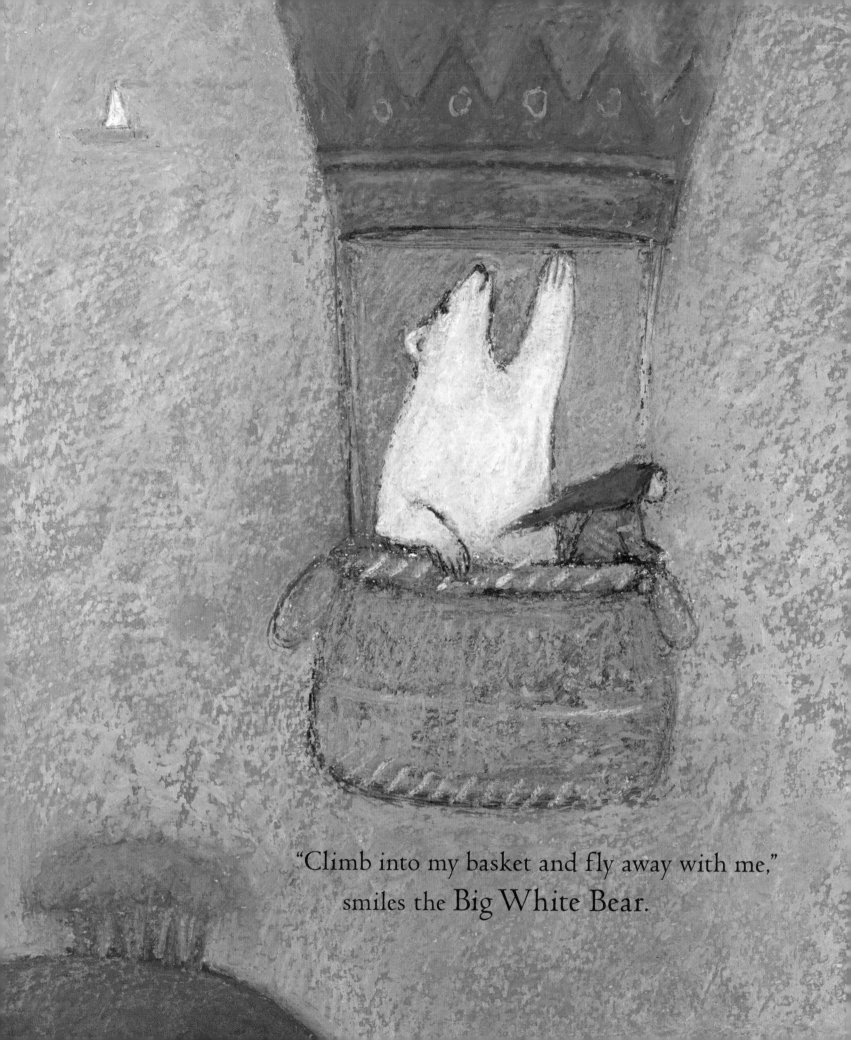

"Climb into my basket and fly away with me,"
smiles the Big White Bear.

"Higher and higher, up through the clouds,
up to the planets, up to the stars.
This side is Venus, that side is Mars.
Away to the north, away to the snow
where the sky sings songs
and the Giant Stag goes."

The Giant Stag cries,
"Climb onto my back,
ride away with me.
We must climb a high hill
to find the Star Tree."

Mia and the Giant Stag gallop
    up the icy path, through the fragrant trees,
past the prowling wolf
    and the mountain hare
        to the very top of the high hill....

The Star Tree shimmers and sparkles
in the glittering night.
And as the snow falls
and the stars bloom
and the sky shines,
Mia plucks
one
small
star
from the gleaming tree.

And as the snow falls and the sky sings,
Mia holds her star and the Great White Goose
comes to take her home.
Away they fly, down from the high hill of stars
and the fragrant trees.
Back across the vast ocean and the Big White Bear's island.

Away from the boat and the Little Red Hare.
Homeward along the river's silver pathway.
Up and over the drowsy land, over the hills,
over the church with the blunted weather vane
that barely stirs in the still air.

Over the rooftops, over the gardens
and back in through the moonlit window.

In the still, quiet room in the sleeping house,
the beautiful horse with a golden mane
shines in the moonlight.
Magical.
Waiting.
Ready.

It is midnight at Midsummer.

The night-light glimmers, star-like.

Mia is asleep.

Tick.
The house breathes in.
Tock.
The house breathes out.

Also illustrated by Catherine Hyde for
FRANCES LINCOLN CHILDREN'S BOOKS

Little Evie in the Wild Wood

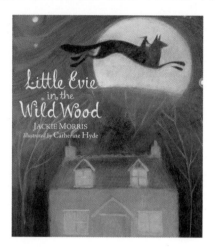

by Jackie Morris
illustrated by Catherine Hyde

When Little Evie follows the path into the wild wood she sees butterflies dancing, hears the rustle of beetles, and listens as the woodpigeons call a soft-voiced warning. What will Little Evie find in the clearing at the heart of the wild wood?

Inspired by fairy tale, this is a beautiful, mysterious story, with evocative pictures and a delicious surprise....

ISBN 978-1-84780-673-4

Frances Lincoln titles are available from all good bookshops.
You can also buy books and find out more about your favourite titles,
authors and illustrators on our website: www.franceslincoln.com